This vacation Bible school inspired the Bible Buddy named Beacon. Beacon is a toucan. In God's creation, toucans have bright beaks that look big and heavy. Beacon reminds kids they don't need to carry big, heavy worries because Jesus rescues.

How cool is that?

Best of Buddies
A Flurry of Worry
Written by **JEFF WHITE**   *Illustrated by* **ROGÉRIO COELHO**

Copyright © 2018 Group Publishing, Inc./0000 0001 0362 4853
Lifetree™ is an imprint of Group Publishing, Inc.
Visit our website: group.com

Library of Congress Cataloging-in-Publication Data

Names: White, Jeff, 1968- author. | Coelho, Rogério, illustrator.
Title: A flurry of worry / written by Jeff White ; illustrated by Rogério
   Coelho.
Description: Loveland, Colorado : Group Publishing, Inc., [2018] | Series:
   Best of buddies
Identifiers: LCCN 2017021760 (print) | LCCN 2017037727 (ebook) | ISBN
   9781470750442 (ePub) | ISBN 9781470750312 (hardcover)
Classification: LCC PZ7.1.W443 (ebook) | LCC PZ7.1.W443 Fl 2018 (print) | DDC
   [E]--dc23
LC record available at https://lccn.loc.gov/2017021760

ISBN: 978-1-4707-5031-2 (hardcover)
ISBN: 978-1-4707-5044-2 (ePub)
Printed in China. 001 China 0118

10 9 8 7 6 5 4 3 2 1   27 26 25 24 23 22 21 20 19 18

Beacon the toucan is going to camp on the beach with his best friends. They'll have a campfire with marshmallows, make midnight sandcastles under the full moon, and fall asleep to the sound of the rolling waves. So much fun!

But Beacon is worried.

His backpack is full, but what if he runs out of marshmallows?

He stuffs a few extra marshmallows into his great big beak, just to be safe.

But Beacon is still worried.

"I'm not worried," says Beacon.
"Just a little…concerned. What if I
can't find any shells on the beach?"

He stores a handful of shells in his beak,
just in case. Lots of room in there!

But Beacon is still worried.

"I'm not worried. Just a tiny bit…bothered. What if I get cold in the cool ocean breezes?"

He crams a thick wool hat and socks into his beak. And a scarf, too!

But Beacon is still worried.

"I'm not worried. Just a little…worked up. What if I get extra thirsty? I can't drink the salty ocean water."

Beacon slides a big bottle full of water into his beak—no, three water bottles—because every drop counts.

But Beacon is still worried.

"I'm not worried. Just a wee bit…bugged. What if it gets too dark? What if the clouds cover the full moon and I can't see?"

Beacon finds his biggest, brightest flashlight and puts it in his beak.

Beacon's beak is starting to feel heavy.

But Beacon is still worried.

"I'm not worried," Beacon says again. "Just a tad troubled. What if I run out of things to talk about with my friends?"

He stuffs a radio and some games into his beak.

But Beacon is still worried.

"I'm not worried. Just kind of…anxious. What if I get bored?"

He crams a couple of his favorite storybooks into his beak.

But Beacon still feels worried.

"I'm not worried," says Beacon. "But I do feel a few butterflies in my tummy. What if I forget my toothbrush?"

He puts a few extra toothbrushes and two tubes of toothpaste into his beak, just in case.

But Beacon is still worried.

"I'm not worried. Just a little restless.
What if I get lost? What if it rains?
What if I get wet?"

He packs a map, an umbrella,
and two extra towels in his beak.

Hrrmmpph.

Uh-oh. Now Beacon is running late. He needs to get to the beach! But his beak is so heavy.

"I hope I've got enough stuff," Beacon mumbles through his overstuffed beak. His head is dizzy with worry.

Beacon gets to the beach, barely able to keep his head up straight. He empties his beak on the beach and falls over.

"Whew!" Beacon says. "I hope I didn't forget anything!"

His friends shake their heads.

"You worry about so many things," says Guac the iguana.

"But only one thing really matters!" says Moe the sloth.

"Being together!" says Hope the jaguar.

"Worry is a heavy burden. Next time, let God do the worrying for you!" Hope says.

Beacon raises his head and smiles at his friends. He feels better already!

"Do not worry about everyday life."
(Matthew 6:25)